Sleepover at the
Haunted Museum

★ Also by ★
Debbie Dadey

MERMAID TALES

BOOK 1: *TROUBLE AT TRIDENT ACADEMY*

BOOK 2: *BATTLE OF THE BEST FRIENDS*

BOOK 3: *A WHALE OF A TALE*

BOOK 4: *DANGER IN THE DEEP BLUE SEA*

BOOK 5: *THE LOST PRINCESS*

BOOK 6: *THE SECRET SEA HORSE*

BOOK 7: *DREAM OF THE BLUE TURTLE*

BOOK 8: *TREASURE IN TRIDENT CITY*

BOOK 9: *A ROYAL TEA*

BOOK 10: *A TALE OF TWO SISTERS*

BOOK 11: *THE POLAR BEAR EXPRESS*

Coming Soon

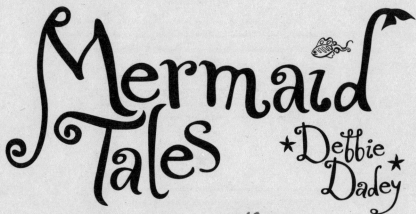

Mermaid Tales

★Debbie Dadey★

Illustrated by
Tatevik Avakyan

BOOK 21

Sleepover at the Haunted Museum

ALADDIN

NEW YORK   LONDON   TORONTO   SYDNEY   NEW DELHI

ALADDIN

An imprint of Simon & Schuster Children's Publishing Division

1230 Avenue of the Americas, New York, New York 10020

First Aladdin paperback edition June 2021

Text copyright © 2021 by Debbie Dadey

Illustrations copyright © 2021 by Tatevik Avakyan

Also available in an Aladdin hardcover edition.

All rights reserved, including the right of reproduction in whole or in part in any form.

ALADDIN and related logo are registered trademarks of Simon & Schuster, Inc.

For information about special discounts for bulk purchases, please contact Simon & Schuster Special Sales at 1-866-506-1949 or business@simonandschuster.com.

The Simon & Schuster Speakers Bureau can bring authors to your live event.

For more information or to book an event contact the Simon & Schuster Speakers Bureau at 1-866-248-3049 or visit our website at www.simonspeakers.com.

Cover designed by Tiara Iandiorio and Jess LaGreca

Interior designed by Michael Rosamilia

The text of this book was set in BelucianNG.

Manufactured in the United States of America 0521 OFF

2 4 6 8 10 9 7 5 3 1

Library of Congress Cataloging-in-Publication Data

Names: Dadey, Debbie, author. | Avakyan, Tatevik, 1983– illustrator.

Title: Sleepover at the haunted museum / Debbie Dadey; illustrated by Tatevik Avakyan.

Description: New York: Aladdin, 2021. | Series: Mermaid tales; 21 | Audience: Ages 6 to 9. | Summary: A young mermaid's friends turn her small birthday party/sleepover into a big extravaganza, complete with a scavenger hunt, scary stories, crafts, a makeup session, and "glow-in-the-dark Shell Wars."

Identifiers: LCCN 2020027508 (print) | LCCN 2020027509 (eBook) |

ISBN 9781534457331 (hardcover) | ISBN 9781534457324 (paperback) |

ISBN 9781534457348 (eBook)

Subjects: CYAC: Mermaids—Fiction. | Birthdays—Fiction. | Parties—Fiction. | Sleepovers—Fiction.

Classification: LCC PZ7.D128 Sl 2021 (print) | LCC PZ7.D128 (eBook) | DDC [Fic]—dc23

LC record available at https://lccn.loc.gov/2020027508

LC eBook record available at https://lccn.loc.gov/2020027509

For Isaac

Cast of Characters

Shelly

Echo

Kiki

Pearl

Rocky

Contents

1

Birthday Party

SHELLY SIREN SWAM AS FAST AS she could. She couldn't wait to tell her best merfriend the exciting news. "Echo!"

Echo Reef stopped practicing her flips outside her small shell home. "What's up?"

Shelly came to a halt so quickly her

long red hair swirled around her face. "Grandfather Siren said I could have you and Kiki sleep over for my birthday."

"Fin-tastic," Echo said, grabbing her book bag to head to school. "It'll be so fun. Let's tell Kiki."

They swam through MerPark toward Trident Academy. Their merbuddy Kiki Coral stayed in a dorm, since her family lived far away in the Eastern Oceans. They found Kiki in the school's huge front hallway.

Shelly barely looked at the colorful carvings of famous merpeople on the ceiling of the huge clamshell. Her birthday was only a few days away. Would Kiki be able to get permission from her parents in time? Maybe they could send a note through the Black Marlin Express.

After they told Kiki the news, Shelly told them, "Grandfather Siren and I usually make pizza for my birthday."

"Splashing!" Echo said. "I know some scary stories to tell before we go to sleep. My aunt told me some good ones."

Kiki pushed back her long black hair. "For one of my brother's parties, we had a scavenger hunt. We searched all over for things on a list. The first one to find everything won a prize."

"Ooh, that would be totally wavy," Shelly said. The scavenger hunt sounded fun, but she wasn't so sure about the scary stories.

Echo slapped her pink tail on the marble floor. "This is going to be the best birthday party ever!"

"OOOH, I want to come." A mergirl from their third-grade classroom stopped beside them.

"I'm sorry, Pearl," Shelly said, feeling embarrassed. She shouldn't have mentioned the party at school. "My grandfather is only letting me have two merfriends sleep over. He's busy making a new exhibit."

Pearl Swamp rolled her eyes. "That's not fair. I invited you to my party!"

Shelly sighed. That wasn't exactly true. Shelly had gone to Pearl's party, but only because she'd filled in for a sick singer in the band. "I will ask my grandfather."

Pearl danced in a circle on the tip of her gold tail. "I love parties. If you had it in the museum, you could invite every mergirl in our class. There's plenty of room!" Shelly's grandfather ran the famed People Museum, and they lived in an apartment above it.

Echo squealed. She collected human things and spent hours looking at the exhibits. "Just think how scary the stories will be with the lights off!"

Shelly was so shocked she didn't know what to say. She didn't like going into the museum when it was dark. In fact, it gave her the creeps! Besides, her grandfather hadn't agreed to a big party. This was a birthday disaster!

Carried Away

WHO CAN NAME A creature that makes glowing mucus?" Mrs. Karp asked her third-grade class later that day.

Rocky Ridge laughed. "Isn't mucus the same as snot?"

Mrs. Karp peered over her half glasses. "Yes, and I expect someone to be able to answer this question. It was in last night's reading assignment."

Shelly tried to remember, but she could only think of the anglerfish's gleaming lure. She was pretty sure the anglerfish didn't have glowing snot. It was hard to focus when she was worried about her birthday party.

Kiki slowly raised her hand. "Doesn't the mauve stinger jellyfish have shining mucus?"

"Yes!" Mrs. Karp cheered. "I'm glad someone did their homework. Now, who knows a fish that uses lights to hide from other fish?"

Shelly thought it might be the dragonfish,

but when Adam answered, she was glad she hadn't raised her hand. "The hatchetfish does that," he said.

"Mervelous!" Mrs. Karp said. "After lunch, we'll do a bit more review and then discuss your next science project."

"Can I use snot in my project?" Rocky asked.

Mrs. Karp nodded. "Perhaps. Now, let's line up for lunch."

When Shelly, Kiki, and Echo were seated at their polished granite lunch table, Shelly spurted out, "What am I going to do? Pearl wants to invite every mergirl in our class to my party."

"Pearl is trying to take over like she always does," Echo told Shelly.

Kiki shrugged. "Pearl does get carried away sometimes. You'll just have to tell her the truth."

"I tried to," Shelly said. "It's not that I wouldn't like to invite everyone, but I don't think Grandfather will let me."

Kiki chewed a bite of her baked sea potato before saying, "You could ask him. If he says no, then Pearl will have to understand."

"That's a good idea," Shelly agreed, and dipped a little octopus leg in spicy lugworm sauce. She always felt better when she had a plan.

Pearl stopped by their table. "Guess what? I think my dad can get a beluga whale to come to your party, and I know

a great bakery. They make cakes that are taller than you with oysters inside! And don't worry about the rest of the entertainment. I will make a list of everything and how much it will cost!"

Pearl floated off to sit with Wanda Slug, leaving Shelly with her mouth wide open. Her grandfather always made her cake, and she'd never even seen a beluga whale.

Echo shook her head. "I think we may be in big trouble."

Party Planning

FTER SCHOOL, SHELLY invited Echo, Pearl, and Kiki to her apartment at the People Museum. They needed to talk about her birthday. After they grabbed a snack of seaweed juice and cuttlefish candy, Pearl slapped a business card on

the kitchen table. "I'm a professional party planner and I have lots of tail-kicking ideas for your birthday party."

"This is for wedding planning." Echo picked up the kelp card.

Pearl twisted her long pearl necklace around a finger. "A party is a party. I think we should have rabbitfish steak for dinner and some coconut shakes. They're a bit expensive, but I can probably get a discount for you."

Shelly splashed up from the table. "Wait just a merminute! We don't have many shells to spend on this party. We have to keep it simple."

Pearl slumped back onto her rock chair and pouted. "I was just trying to help."

Kiki patted Pearl's shoulder. "We need to remember that this is Shelly's birthday. First, we have to find out if her grandfather will even let her invite every mergirl in the class."

"If he does, I'll be in charge of storytelling," Echo volunteered. Shelly hoped she could talk her friend out of telling a scary story.

"I can plan a scavenger hunt," Kiki said. "Shelly, you won't have to do a thing."

Shelly crossed her arms before looking at Pearl and saying, "Grandfather and I should take care of the food."

Pearl sat up straight. "I can take care of all the other activities if your grandfather agrees."

"Okay, but they can't cost much," Shelly warned Pearl.

Pearl nodded. "They will be free, or just a few shells."

"Thanks," Shelly said. "Now comes the hard part. I have to ask Grandfather. Wish me luck." Shelly didn't want to disappoint Pearl, but she really didn't want to sleep in the museum! When she was a little fry, she'd had nightmares about great white sharks chasing her around the storage room. Even though she knew the noises from the room were just the creaking of the old ship, they still gave her the creeps!

"Good luck," Kiki, Echo, and Pearl said as Shelly left the apartment to visit her grandfather's office in the museum. They waited. And waited. And waited! Still Shelly didn't come back.

"What could be taking so long?" Pearl asked.

Echo shrugged. "Maybe her grandfather doesn't like the idea of a big party."

"I should go back to my dorm room and start on my school project," Kiki said.

Echo sighed. "We do have a lot of homework."

Pearl frowned. "Let's wait just a little longer."

Finally Shelly swam into the kitchen. Kiki, Echo, and Pearl gathered around. "What did your grandfather say?" Echo asked.

Terrible Surprise

BEST P-PARTY EVER," MORGAN said softly before taking a bite of shrimp pizza.

"I'm glad you could come." Shelly meant it. Her grandfather had surprised her by allowing such a big party. It had taken every bit of the last couple of days to get

ready, but she was glad all the mergirls in her class could come. She just wished they could have fit into her apartment instead of the Grand Hall of the People Museum, surrounded by sunken boats and something called cars. Humans must be silly to lose things so big!

No one was looking at boats or cars now though. All around her, mergirls from her class lounged on kelp rugs while eating their dinner. It'd been fun making three different kinds of pizza and sand hopper chips with her grandfather before the party. Grandfather Siren had talked in a funny accent and spun a pizza on his fingertips to make her laugh. That had been totally wavy.

She needed to remember to thank him again.

Shelly leaned over to Echo. "I thought this would be a disaster with so many merkids, but it's shell-tastic!" Shelly had been worried about nothing; she hadn't been scared at all with her merfriends around.

Echo took a big slurp of coconut shake. "Just wait until I tell my story. It is super scary!"

Shelly put down her pizza and glanced at the storage room door. "Do you know any funny stories?" Funny sounded better.

Echo frowned. "But you'll love this one!"

Shelly wanted to say more, but she didn't get a chance because Pearl appeared on the stage. A stoplight loose-jaw fish shone on her. "Merladies, it is time to unveil the most splash-errific cake ever!"

Every mergirl swam closer to the stage to see Pearl and a seaweed-covered table. The cake under the sea-weed cloth had to be huge. Shelly hoped Pearl hadn't gone crazy and spent too many shells on it. This would be her first birthday cake that her grandfather hadn't made.

"Wait!" Kiki said. "We need to sing the birthday song first."

Shelly smiled as her merfriends sang together,

"We wish you happy birthday
the merfolk way,
fins up . . . fins down,
with a big smack and a mighty sound!"

Shelly laughed as every mergirl splashed her in the traditional birthday song.

Pearl tapped one of her gold fins on the stage. "Now can we have the cake?"

"Sure! Thanks for getting it and the coconut shakes." Shelly swallowed the last bite of her pizza.

"You are going to be so surprised." Pearl giggled.

"Just show us," Echo said.

With a sweep of her hand, Pearl pulled the cover away. Shelly was stunned. So was every mergirl. They all screamed and swam for their lives!

5

Eels and Pillows

FOR SHARK'S SAKE! WHY IN the ocean would you put eels in a cake?" Echo asked Pearl.

Shelly shivered. Eels weren't usually scary, but she'd been so startled she'd screamed along with every other mergirl. The museum had been a frenzy of squealing girls and swarming eels!

Pearl twisted her long necklace. "I read in a *MerStyle* magazine that kings and queens used to put eels in their pies. I thought since you're a princess, you should have them too."

Shelly sighed. Most of the time she forgot that she was related to Queen Edwina, but Pearl never forgot. Seeing eels slither out of a cake had scared the seaweed out of Shelly. Still, Pearl had meant well, so Shelly said, "Don't get your tail in a knot. All the eels are outside now."

Even with the eels gone, no one ate much cake. Shelly forced herself to eat most of her piece. She didn't want to hurt Pearl's feelings.

"Now let's make friendship bracelets," Pearl said, bringing out a huge shell full of colorful seaweed strands and sparkling beads. "It's easy!"

After Pearl told everyone what to do, Shelly gave it a try. It wasn't easy for her!

"I'm done!" Kiki said, raising her arm to show a perfectly braided bracelet to match her purple tail.

"Me too," Echo said. "I'm going to make another."

Shelly groaned. Her fingers didn't do what they were supposed to, and her seaweed was in knots. "I'm going to make sure everyone has a pillow for tonight," she said, hiding the bracelet behind her back.

Wanda giggled and bopped Shelly

across the tummy. "I have my pillow!"

As fast as a sailfish, the other mer-girls finished their bracelets and grabbed their lichen pillows. "Pillow fight!" yelled Kiki.

Shelly joined in the fun and bopped Pearl on her head. All around them, mer-girls squealed with excitement. Shelly was enjoying her party again.

"AHHHHHH!"

Shelly dropped her pillow and swirled around. Someone was not having fun.

"Oh, Wanda, I-I'm so sorry." Morgan looked ready to cry, and Wanda was hold-ing her bloody nose.

"Come with me," Shelly told Wanda. "Don't worry, Morgan, it's just a nosebleed.

Tell Kiki to start the scavenger hunt, and we'll be right back."

Shelly took Wanda up to her apartment and put a cold blue sponge on Wanda's nose. It took quite a while for the bleeding to stop. Luckily, Grandfather Siren suggested pinching her nose, and that finally worked.

"Let's get back to the party," Wanda said. "We don't want to miss anything."

"Oh my Neptune, I'm glad you're back," Kiki said when Shelly and Wanda swam into the Grand Hall.

"What's wrong?" Shelly asked.

Kiki wiped away a tear. "Echo is missing!"

6

Lost

WHAT HAPPENED?" SHELLY asked.

Kiki took a deep breath. "Echo disappeared at the end of our scavenger hunt."

"It—it was right after I saw a strange glowing light in the storage room," Morgan stammered as all the other mergirls gathered behind her. "I was so scared I left the lights on! Echo may have gone in afterward."

Shelly glanced at the storage room. All the girls had stashed their overnight bags inside the big room, but the door was closed now. "Did anyone look in the storage room?" Shelly's heart beat faster. What had Morgan seen? What if Echo was trapped inside with a shark? Or something worse?

"That was the first place I checked," Pearl said, and Shelly's chest didn't thump quite as hard.

Wanda squeezed Shelly's shoulder. "This museum is huge. She could be lost forever! Or maybe a hammerhead shark ate her!"

Several mergirls whimpered, and Morgan gasped. "I want to go home be-before I get lost or eaten too."

"Don't be a scaredy-slug," Pearl muttered. "There aren't any sharks in here." Everyone glanced around the big hall. It wasn't all that long ago that a great white shark had invaded their school.

Shelly tried not to look worried, but it was strange for Echo to vanish into thin water. Still, Echo loved to explore the museum. She had to be inside somewhere! "I'm sure Echo is checking out a human exhibit. You know how much she likes people stuff."

"But we've looked all over," Kiki said. "My scavenger hunt was a terrible idea. I'm so sorry."

Shelly didn't want Kiki to feel bad. "No, a scavenger hunt was a great idea."

"It was fun until Echo ruined it." Pearl put her hands on her hips. "Why would Echo swim off like that and not tell anyone? It's so rude!"

Kiki snapped her fingers. "I just remembered. Didn't your grandfather make a new exhibit?"

Shelly hugged Kiki. "That's right! It's not open yet, but Echo might have figured out how to sneak inside."

In one big wave, the mergirls followed Shelly to the new exhibit. Sure enough, Echo floated beside a strange table with holes in the corners and sides. She rolled a white ball on the tabletop and it whacked into a red ball. It slammed into a corner hole.

"Echo!" Shelly was glad Echo was safe, but she couldn't help being a little mad at her merfriend for scaring everyone.

"Don't you know we've been looking all over for you?" Pearl shouted.

"Oh, I'm so sorry. I found this new human thingy and I had to try it out." Echo's cheeks turned red.

Shelly hoped nothing else would go wrong at her party. "I'm tired," she said. "I think we should all go to sleep now."

"You have to open presents, and then we can sleep," Wanda suggested.

"We can't." Pearl slapped her gold tail on the museum floor. "I was in charge of games, and we haven't finished yet. The last one is the best. After presents, we'll do one more game."

"And don't forget my scary story," Echo reminded them.

Shelly sighed. She wasn't terribly tired, but she wasn't sure how much more fun she could take!

7

Stinky Stuff

SHELLY CROSSED HER TAIL FINS
after thanking her merfriends
for their lovely presents. She
really wanted to play a splashing game
of Shell Wars. The big main room in the
museum gave them plenty of space to
toss a shell around and try to get it into

a goal. It would be shelltacular!

Pearl's eyes sparkled when she announced, "It's time for beauty make-overs!"

"What?" Shelly gasped. "That's not a game!"

Wanda giggled. "It is to me. Let's do it!"

Before Shelly could stop them, her merfriends had wound her hair into a tall, tall spiral on top of her head. It looked just like a crooked nautilus shell. Shelly didn't want to hurt anyone's feel-ings, but she looked ridiculous!

"You're wave-tastic!" Echo squealed.

Shelly shrugged. She didn't look any sillier than anyone else. All the mer-girls had hairdos sticking up in every direction. Pearl's hair looked like a turkey fish's wild fins.

"Next is makeup!" Pearl giggled.

Shelly shook her head, and her tall hair wiggled from side to side. "We're too young for makeup."

Pearl nodded. "Usually, but your grandfather said we could do it for fun tonight."

Shelly's head started hurting. Makeup and fancy hairdos were not for her. Why couldn't they just play Shell Wars?

"Put makeup on Shelly first," Echo said. "After all, it is her birthday."

Shelly was surprised anyone remembered, but she sat perfectly still while Pearl and Echo smeared all kinds of goop on her

face. Some of it smelled good and some reeked.

"What is that terrible odor?" Shelly gasped.

"Oh, that's just the anchovy base." Wanda rubbed some of the stinky stuff on her own face.

"Ew, get that away from me," Kiki said, holding her nose.

Shelly hoped she wouldn't throw up. "Are you almost done?" she asked.

Pearl turned Shelly away from the mirror and used a sea lily to dab something cool on her cheeks. It actually felt good. "I just want to add a little jellyfish jelly and ponyfish powder," Pearl told her.

"Ta-da!" Pearl glided back to reveal

Shelly's makeup. Everyone floated in silence. Kiki looked at Echo. Echo looked at Pearl.

"Well," Shelly said. "How do I look?"

Finally Wanda answered, "You look mervelous!"

Shelly twisted to look in the big mirror at the end of the hall. She couldn't believe what she saw!

Hideous Creature

SHELLY HAD NEVER SEEN ANY-
thing so strange. Her cheeks
were neon orange and her lips
were bright purple. With her hair in silly
swirls and glittering blue patches above
her eyes, she looked like a wild parrotfish.

"Do you like it?" Pearl asked quietly.

Shelly giggled. "It's definitely interesting."

Pearl laughed as well. "I might have gotten a little carried away with the purple lips."

"A little?" Echo snickered. "She looks like a lunchroom disaster."

"It's not that bad," Kiki told them. "I kind of like the hair."

Shelly patted her tall, tall hair. As long as she lived, she would certainly never forget this wild birthday party. "Now it's your turn."

Shelly put ponyfish powder on Morgan while all around them mergirls took turns applying makeup to one another. Nobody's lips were quite as purple as Shelly's, though.

Shelly laughed to see Kiki with an

orange nose and Pearl with blue cheeks. Before long everyone was doing a pretend fashion show with silly voices and swimming in zany ways.

Finally Echo clapped her hands. "It's scary story time! I'm going to put on my costume."

Shelly reached out to beg Echo not to frighten them, but her merfriend was too fast. Wanda grabbed Shelly's arm and asked, "Why does she need a costume to tell a story?"

Shelly shrugged, hoping the story wasn't too creepy. She glanced at the storage room door—thankfully, it was shut tight. Her wild makeup was already enough to give her nightmares!

All the mergirls settled in front of the

stage. Pearl pulled open the curtains. In the middle of the stage was the most hideous creature Shelly had ever seen. All the mergirls gasped.

"It's a stonefish!" Kiki shouted.

"Ahh! Th-those are poisonous," Morgan squealed.

"Let's get out of here!" several mergirls screamed.

"Wait!" Echo said, only the voice came from the stonefish. "It's just me."

"Wow," Pearl said. "That's a great costume."

The stonefish/Echo nodded its stone head. "My sister, Crystal, helped me make it."

"It looks so real," Shelly admitted. In

fact, she wished it didn't look quite so life-like. Or so nightmarelike!

"And now," Echo said in a deep voice. "Get ready to be afraid."

"Too late," Shelly whispered.

Haunted Ship

KIKI SQUEEZED SHELLY'S hand tight. Echo's voice was practically a whisper as she told of a haunted sunken boat. "Every wrong turn inside the deserted ship got the lost mergirl deeper and deeper into the darkness. Finally she could barely see her tail."

Morgan whimpered. Pearl and Wanda cuddled together and shivered. Shelly didn't like being afraid. Usually she was pretty brave, but she liked funny stories better than scary ones. Why couldn't Echo tell a silly story? Thankfully, no one had turned off the lights. Shelly's blue tail tapped the floor. She was trembling!

Echo's voice got deeper. "To this day, the mergirl is still looking for a way out. Would you like to know where that ship is?"

Shelly shook her head, but Wanda asked, "Where?"

"You are on the very same ship!" Echo's voice got even spookier.

Gasps and squeals rang out around Shelly. The People Museum was housed in an overturned human vessel. "Every night, the mermaid wanders, her eyes glowing with sadness," Echo moaned.

"Uh . . . oh, I saw something shining in the storage room!" Morgan shrieked. Every eye turned toward the closed door. A couple of mergirls sobbed.

"It's all right," Shelly said, trying to calm everyone down. "The museum isn't haunted." At least she hoped it wasn't. Now she really would hate to go into the storage room!

"But all is not lost. There is one thing that can save her. And it's coming now," Echo said in a loud voice.

"Now?" Kiki squeaked as Echo continued.

"Through the gloom, a huge shape appears. It's getting closer and closer!"

"Is . . . is it a bad merguy?" Morgan asked.

Wanda put her hands over her ears. "I can't listen."

"It is . . ." Echo paused.

"A shark?" Pearl whispered.

"A stonefish?" Shelly asked.

Echo shook her head.

Shelly gulped and Kiki squeezed her hand tighter.

"It is . . . a clown fish with a huge party hat!" Echo shouted as she hopped out of the stonefish costume wearing a pointed hat. "Happy birthday, Shelly!"

All the mergirls laughed. Shelly

smiled. At least the story had a happy ending.

"What's that?" Pearl squealed and pointed toward the hall.

A dark shape loomed in the doorway. "Eeeek!" everyone screamed.

"Merladies, it's just me." Grandfather Siren held up a lanternfish to show his face. "I think you've had enough scary stories for one night. Now it's time to get some sleep."

Several mergirls groaned, but Shelly was glad to lie down on her kelp mat. All the excitement had worn her out. She couldn't wait to get some rest.

Kiki lay down beside Shelly. "That was creepy. I thought something horrible was going to happen."

Shelly nodded. She wanted to forget about the story.

"It was too real for me," Pearl said. "One time I actually was trapped in a haunted ship. I thought I was going to die."

"We tried to stop you," Echo spoke up.

"I never dreamed you would really go inside," Shelly admitted. Pearl had been hunting for treasure, but it had been way too dangerous to go into an old rotting ship.

Pearl sighed. "It was a silly thing to do. I almost died of fright when I saw that blackdevil fish."

"I'll never go on a real haunted ship," Echo told them. Everyone agreed and settled down on their mats. Echo's mat was right beside Shelly's.

"Good night and sweet dreams," Grandfather Siren said as he tapped the glowing jellyfish and lanternfish lights off and left for his apartment upstairs. Several mergirls giggled in the darkness, but then it became quiet. Deathly quiet.

Shelly tried to go to sleep. She turned to the left. She flipped her tail this way and that. It didn't do any good. She couldn't stop thinking about the scary story.

She listened for any strange sounds coming from the storage room. Morgan muttered in her sleep, and someone snored softly, but there were no creepy noises. Whew!

Surely Shelly could go to sleep now. Finally she turned to the right. She couldn't believe her eyes!

She sat straight up. Something must have escaped from the storage room! It stared at her in the darkness. Something horrible!

Glowing Eyes

HAUNTED EYES GLOWED AT
Shelly in the darkness. Was
it the lost mermaid from
the story? Was it a monster? If Shelly
moved, would something eat her? Slowly,
she reached out for her merfriends. Kiki
was too far away to touch with her left

hand, so Shelly tapped Echo with her right.

Echo didn't wake up. In fact, she murmured in her sleep. "Echo," Shelly said, patting her again, harder this time.

Echo rolled over onto Shelly's arm. "Ouch, get off!" Shelly whispered. Echo didn't move!

Shelly jiggled her arm and muttered, "Echo, wake up."

Oh no! Now there were two sets of glowing eyes. There must have been a whole family of monsters in the storage room! Shelly screeched.

All around the big room, mergirls scrambled in the darkness and screamed. Kiki turned on a jellyfish lamp, and the glowing eyes disappeared.

Pearl yawned and stretched. "What's going on? I need my beauty sleep."

Shelly sprang onto the tip of her blue tail and glanced around. The storage room door was shut tight! "Where did the eyes go?"

Pearl frowned. "What in the ocean are you talking about?"

"Didn't you see those spooky-looking eyes?" Shelly asked.

Several mergirls nodded. "They were the creepiest ever!" Wanda agreed.

Morgan sobbed. "It . . . it was the lost mermaid!"

Pearl shook her head. "You're imagining things. No more scary stories tonight! Let's turn off the light and get some sleep."

Shelly lay back down. She had been thinking about the story. Maybe Pearl was right. Kiki turned off the light and immediately the menacing eyes reappeared. Only this time, there wasn't just one set of eyes. There weren't just two sets. Eyes were everywhere!

All the mergirls screamed, and Kiki

turned the light back on. The eyes disappeared again. "Something strange is going on here!" Shelly snapped.

"You don't think Rocky and Adam are playing tricks on us, do you?" Echo asked.

It did seem like the kind of prank Rocky would play, but how could he have gotten inside? Grandfather Siren always locked the building at night to keep unwanted sea creatures from drifting in.

"No," Shelly told her merfriends. "I saw Grandfather bolt the door."

"Th-that only leaves one other explanation," Morgan whispered.

"What's that?" Shelly asked.

Wanda's eyes grew wide. "The People Museum is haunted!"

Pearl shook her head. "There are no such things as ghosts!"

"Something must be in the storage room. That's where Morgan saw the strange light," Shelly gasped. "Whatever it was probably hid when Pearl looked." Shelly's nightmares were coming true, only something worse than sharks were in there. Unless Wanda was right and instead of sea monsters, there were ghosts. And instead of one mermaid ghost, there was a whole horde of them! Had they opened and closed the door to sneak out? Of course, ghosts could go right through doors!

Morgan put a fin in her mouth while Wanda looked ready to cry. Pearl hopped out of bed and slapped her gold tail on the floor. "Sweet seaweed, let's just look in the storage room."

"Of course," Kiki said. "There must be a reason for all this."

Shelly knew Kiki was probably right, but what if something pounced on them the minute they opened the door? "We should get Grandfather."

"That will take forever," Pearl snapped. "I'm tired now." She whirled across the room and yanked the storage room door open.

"Wait!" Shelly screamed, but it was too late!

Snot

PEARL DISAPPEARED INSIDE
the storage room . . . and she
didn't come out! Several mergirls whimpered when Pearl still didn't
appear.

"Pearl?" Shelly jumped out of her covers
to help her merfriend.

"Pearl!" Echo shouted. "You come out of there right this merminute!"

Pearl peered around the opening and frowned at Echo. "See, it's not nice to disappear without a word."

Echo's cheeks turned red, but Shelly wanted to know what was going on inside the storage room. "Are there any monsters inside there?" she asked.

"Any sh-sharks?" Morgan stammered.

"Ghosts?" Wanda asked.

"No, no, and no," Pearl said. "I checked everywhere!"

"Then what did we see?" Kiki wondered.

"It's so strange," Shelly said. "As soon as the lights come on, the eyes disappear."

"And the creatures attached to those eyes," Wanda whimpered.

"They aren't normal eyes. They glow like they're magical," Echo said.

"Or g-ghostly," Morgan added. Several mergirls squealed and dove under their kelp blankets.

Pearl shook her head and her blond hair swirled around her face. "There must be a reason for such craziness."

"I wonder . . . ," Kiki muttered.

Pearl rolled her eyes. "Don't tell me you believe in ghosts too!"

"No." Kiki swam toward the cluster of beauty supplies stacked just inside the storage room. She picked up a bottle and read silently.

"What are you doing?" Pearl asked. "This isn't the time to put on lipstick. We have to figure out what's going on. I bet Rocky found a way to trick us."

"It wasn't Rocky," Kiki said, handing the bottle to Shelly.

"Well, it's not ghosts," Pearl snapped.

Shelly smiled after reading the label. "There are no ghosts in this museum."

Wanda slapped her red tail on the marble floor. "Sweet seaweed, what's going on?"

"This makeup has vampire squid mucus with syllid fireworm booster in it," Kiki explained.

Several mergirls lifted their heads from under the covers and stared at Kiki with blank looks on their faces. "What does snot have to do with ghosts?" Echo asked.

"Didn't you read your homework assignment?" Shelly asked.

Kiki nodded. "It was about bioluminescence."

"What in the ocean are you talking about?" Echo asked.

"It means they glow in the dark," Shelly said.

Pearl grabbed the bottle from Shelly. "Are you telling me we rubbed squid snot all over our faces?"

Shelly laughed. "Yes, I guess we did."

"Ewww, that's disgusting," Wanda gasped. "Get this stuff off me now!"

Shelly held up a hand. "Wait a minute. I have a great idea."

In the Dark

NO WAVY WAY!" PEARL snapped. "I want to wash this snot off right away!"

"It is Shelly's birthday," Kiki reminded them. "We should do one thing she wants."

Echo put her left hand on her left hip. "Kiki's right. We did the scavenger hunt for Kiki, I wanted a scary story, we did the craft that Pearl wanted, and the makeup Wanda wanted. Shelly should get to play glow-in-the-dark Shell Wars."

"But how can we even see the shell if it's dark?" Wanda asked.

Morgan nodded. "It's bonky barnacles."

"That's the great part," Shelly said, rubbing makeup on a shell. "It'll glow and so will the nets."

Pearl shook her head. "I don't think I'll be any good at this."

Shelly grinned. "It won't matter because it's just for fun."

"And birthday parties are supposed to be shelltacular fun!" Echo said with a wink.

Shelly found a supply of human sticks

with nets at the ends. They were similar to Shell Wars sticks, and everyone rubbed them with vampire-squid-snot makeup. Echo's birthday present, a pretty box, would be the goal. "All right, as soon as Kiki turns off the light and tosses the shell," Shelly told them, "we'll each try to capture the shell and get it in the box first."

Pearl held up her hand. "Wait, I don't want to get smacked in the face. Let's put some of that glowing stuff on our noses too."

"Good idea," Shelly said. "We'd better put some around the edges of the box as well."

When everything was ready, Kiki yelled, "Get ready, get set, lights off!"

For just a second, everyone was still. Strange glowing faces, nets, hands, and eyes filled the dark hall. It was a bit scary, but exciting too. "Here comes the shell," Kiki said.

Immediately, ten nets swished through the water toward the floating shell. Someone's net sent the shell spinning away. All the mergirls squealed and splashed after it.

Shelly laughed and tried to get the shell before anyone else. She accidently caught the head of someone with a glowing green nose. "Yikes, let me go!" Echo yelled.

"Oops, sorry." Shelly giggled.

A loud crash sounded from behind them. Oh no! Was someone hurt?

Suddenly Pearl screamed, "I think I've got it!"

The lights came on and Grandfather Siren frowned at everyone. Wanda's head was stuck inside a little boat, and Morgan was pulling on Wanda's tail to help her out. With a pop, Wanda jerked away from the boat and waved. "Don't worry. I'm fine."

Shelly looked around, and except for Wanda's boat being turned sideways, the rest of the museum looked perfect. "What is going on here?" Grandfather asked. "I heard screaming and all sorts of terrible noises."

Pearl swam up to Grandfather Siren. "We were playing Shell Wars in the dark." She held up the box with the shell inside. "I won!"

"In the dark?" Grandfather shook his head. "Why?"

Kiki swam up to the other side of Grandfather Siren. "Because we wanted to do something special for Shelly, even if it was a bit wacky."

Grandfather rubbed his chin and raised his furry eyebrows. Hopefully he wouldn't be mad. What if he made everyone go home?

Suddenly Grandfather laughed. "Well, I guess there's only one thing left to say."

"Happy birthday?" Echo said softly.

Grandfather nodded. "That and good night. But this time, no more fun and games. It's very late, and you need to get some sleep. And so do I."

After scrubbing their faces, the mergirls called, "Good night!" as Grandfather turned out the lights once more. Shelly snuggled under her kelp blanket. She had a smile on her face. Her birthday disaster had turned out to be a happy birthday after all!

Bioluminescent Creatures and Facts

⭐

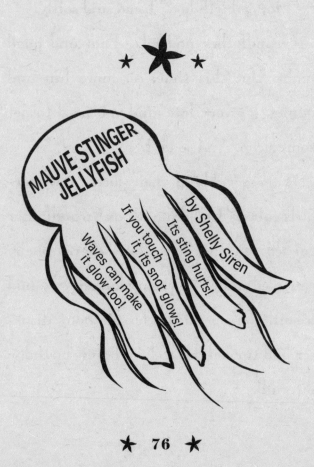

MAUVE STINGER JELLYFISH

by Shelly Siren

Its sting hurts!

If you touch it, its snot glows!

Waves can make it glow too!

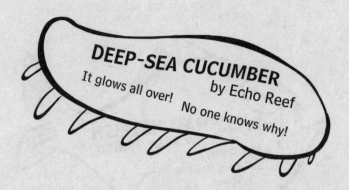

DEEP-SEA CUCUMBER
by Echo Reef

It glows all over! No one knows why!

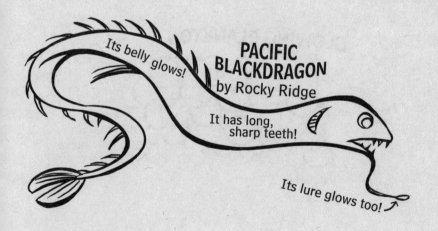

Its belly glows!

PACIFIC BLACKDRAGON
by Rocky Ridge

It has long, sharp teeth!

Its lure glows too!

LOVELY HATCHETFISH
by Pearl Swamp

1. Not lovely
2. Glows to hide
3. Silver
4. Big eyes

GLOWING PLANKTON
by Kiki Coral

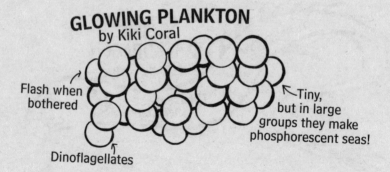

Flash when bothered

↖Tiny, but in large groups they make phosphorescent seas!

Dinoflagellates

★ 78 ★

The Mermaid Song

REFRAIN:

Let the water roar

Deep down we're swimming along

Twirling, swirling, singing the mermaid song.

VERSE 1:

Shelly flips her tail

Racing, diving, chasing a whale

Twirling, swirling, singing the mermaid song.

VERSE 2:

Pearl likes to shine

Oh my Neptune, she looks so fine

Twirling, swirling, singing the mermaid song.

VERSE 3:

Shining Echo flips her tail

Backward and forward without fail

Twirling, swirling, singing the mermaid song.

VERSE 4:

Amazing Kiki

Far from home and floating so free

Twirling, swirling, singing the mermaid song.

Author's Note

I F YOU'VE EVER SEEN A FIREFLY LIGHT up at night, then you have seen an example of bioluminescence. Creatures who glow are rare on land, but in the ocean there are many, many creatures who light up! It is caused by a chemical reaction. Some animals do it to catch their dinner, some light up to scare off enemies, and some do it to attract a mate.

If you get a chance to visit the Smoky Mountains in the southeastern United

States at the end of May, you'll want to see the synchronized fireflies. These amazing creatures blink all together in a totally natural fireworks show!

Glow strong,

Debbie Dadey

Glossary

ANCHOVY: This small silver fish is often eaten by humans in Caesar salads, on toast, and even on pizza!

ANGLERFISH: The deep-sea anglerfish has a sticklike lure on its forehead. Bacteria causes the end of the "stick" to glow.

BARNACLE: Barnacles attach themselves permanently to solid surfaces, like ships or docks. They are related to crabs and lobsters.

BELUGA WHALE: The beluga whale is sometimes called the white whale, as well as the "canary of the seas" because it makes many different sounds (clicks, trills, and chirps).

BLACK MARLIN: Black marlins can weigh up to 1,500 pounds and can go up to eighty miles per hour!

BLACKDEVIL FISH: The deep-sea common blackdevil fish has long sharp teeth and a glowing lure.

BLUE SPONGE: This beautiful sponge is bright blue. The dorid sea slug likes to eat it.

CLAM: The tropical giant clam can be more than three feet wide (the length of a Fruit Roll-Up fruit-flavored snack).

CLOWN FISH: The brightly colored clown fish has a symbiotic relationship with sea anemones. Clown fish have a safe home, and at the same time, they clean the anemones. The anemones even get nutrients from the waste the clown fish produce. Because they both benefit, it is called mutualism.

COCONUT: Coconuts grow on coconut palm trees. Inside the hard shell is coconut milk.

CORAL: Coral reefs are made by small saclike animals. One fourth of all ocean species depend on reefs for food and shelter.

CUTTLEFISH: Cuttlefish are related to octopuses. Cuttlefish can be poisonous to humans.

DEEP SEA CUCUMBER: This cucumber-shaped

creature has peglike legs and lives on the seafloor.

DINOFLAGELLATE: These tiny single-celled organisms can be seen floating together to make a glowing mass in the sea.

DRAGONFISH: This deep-sea fish shines a red light on its prey. Did you know that red light is invisible to most other deep-sea creatures?

EEL: The deep-sea slender snipe eel has jaws that look like a bird's bill.

GREAT WHITE SHARK: The great white is probably the most famous of all sharks, but it is not the biggest. The whale shark (forty-six feet long) and basking shark (thirty-three feet long) are both bigger than the twenty-three-foot-long great white.

HAMMERHEAD SHARK: This shark has an unusually shaped head that looks like a hammer!

JELLYFISH: The moon jellyfish can be found in almost every part of the ocean, except for extremely cold water. It looks a bit like a flying saucer!

KELP: Kelp is large brown algae seaweed. It grows in underwater forests.

LANTERNFISH: The small, spotted lanternfish uses the photophores on its sides and belly to create a light show.

LICHEN: Lichen can be many sizes, shapes, and forms. It is very tough and can grow almost anywhere!

LOVELY HATCHETFISH: The hatchetfish is very thin and is an expert at hiding. It uses bioluminescence to help it hide in the light from above.

LUGWORM: Lugworms eat sand! They leave behind coiled remains for you to find when it is washed ashore.

MAUVE STINGER JELLYFISH: If disturbed, this jellyfish glows with bioluminescence. If it is touched, it makes glowing mucus!

NAUTILUS: The nautilus species has existed for sixty-five million years! It uses jet propulsion to swim. It forces water from its shell to move through the water.

OCTOPUS: The spit of the blue-ringed octopus is strong enough to kill a human! It lives in the tropical west Pacific and Indian Oceans.

OYSTER: The common oyster has nearly

disappeared from the wild because of overexploitation, and now most oysters are commercially farmed.

PACIFIC BLACKDRAGON: This snakelike creature is black on the inside and outside! It has photophores on its belly that light up.

PARROTFISH: This brightly colored fish grinds coral in its sharp teeth to eat the attached algae.

PEARL: Beadlike pearls are formed in oysters when a grain of sand irritates the inside of their shells. They coat the sand with nacre, forming pearls.

PONYFISH: The common ponyfish is silver with a brown back (a bit like a saddle). It can be found off the coast of Australia, and its belly can glow!

RABBITFISH: Rabbitfish are also known as foxfaces. They are usually peaceful, but their spines can sting you!

REEF: These multicolored formations are actually alive!

SAILFISH: The sailfish is considered the fastest fish in the ocean.

SAND HOPPER: This tiny creature loves rotting seaweed and is also known as the sand flea.

SEA LILY: Sea lilies have long stalks with a feathery, flowerlike top.

SEA POTATO: This sea urchin likes to burrow in the sand, and its dried shell looks very much like a baked potato!

SEAWEED: Seaweed is a type of algae. Some people like to eat it.

SHARK: Sharks do not have bones, but have a cartilaginous skeleton (like what supports your nose).

SHELL: Several creatures have shells, including mollusks, barnacles, and horseshoe crabs.

SHRIMP: The peacock mantis shrimp is very colorful and very fast. It can move at seventy-five miles per hour to catch its dinner!

SLUG: Perhaps the opalescent sea slug should be called the porcupine slug. It captures stinging cells from other creatures and stores them in its tentacles. One touch and ouch!

STONEFISH: The stonefish's sting can kill a human! It looks just like a rock and lives in the Indian and western Pacific Oceans.

STOPLIGHT LOOSEJAW FISH: This fish lives in the deep sea and has two light-producing organs to attract dinner.

SYLLID FIREWORM: The female syllid fireworm glows to attract a mate when there is a new moon.

TURKEY FISH: The turkey fish is also called the lionfish. It has red stripes and a painful sting!

VAMPIRE SQUID: When the vampire squid is afraid, it flashes lights and squirts outs mucus that sparkles!

Debbie Dadey

is an award-winning children's book author who has written more than 175 traditionally published books. She is best known for her series the Adventures of the Bailey School Kids, written with Marcia Thornton Jones. Debbie lives with her husband and two dogs in Sevierville, Tennessee. She is not a mermaid . . . yet.

READ & LEARN
with
simon kids

Nancy Drew
✴ CLUE BOOK ✴

MEET JUNIOR MONSTER SCOUTS WOLFY, FRANKY, AND VAMPYRA! CAN THEY BEAT THE CRANKY BARON VON GRUMP AND EARN THEIR MERIT BADGES?

The Monster Squad

Crash! Bang! Boo!

It's Raining Bats and Frogs!

Monster of Disguise

JUL 2021